nds™

www.icelands.com

Pookie™ and Tushka™

find a little piano

written and illustrated by
Jorge Antonio Tello Aliaga
J o r g e

Pers Publishing
Año 0 : Principio

Publisher's Cataloging-in-Publication
(Provided by Quality Books, Inc.)

Jorge.
Pookie and Tushka find a little piano / written and illustrated by Jorge.
p. cm.
SUMMARY: A frozen piano brings a little penguin and a
polar bear cub fun, excitement, and a lesson about
the essence of friendship.
LCCN 2002111937
ISBN 1-932179-23-2

1. Penguins--Juvenile fiction. 2. Polar bear--Juvenile fiction. 3. Friendship--Juvenile fiction.
[1. Penguins--Fiction. 2. Polar bear--Fiction. 3. Friendship--Fiction.]   I. Title.

PZ7.J6872Po 2003   [E]
QBI33-1099

Printed in China
First Edition

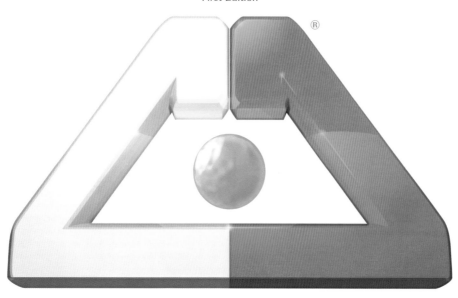

Pers Publishing
5255 Stevens Creek Blvd. # 232-A, Santa Clara, CA 95051

Meet Pookie and Tushka, learn Cool Facts, and journey through the Icelands at:
w w w . p e r s . c o m

Special thanks to:
Dave Valiulis for helping with the editing of this book.
The people at Palace Press International.

This book was put together using Adobe® InDesign® software on a Power Macintosh G4 (with a huge 23" Apple Cinema HD Display ☺)
The illustrations on this book were created with watercolors and pencils, then processed with Adobe® Photoshop® software to make then look extra cool (no pun intended).

Los Tiempos antes de Principio han terminado

To Alikito:
For the inspiration for Pookie and Tushka.
I've grown so much because of you, little Alechka.

To Frederickito:
For becoming the brother I always wished for.
Thank you for ALWAYS being so good to me.

To Stevecito:
For being my bestestest buddy in the whole world.
For having the heart and soul of a little kid.
(Steve Sanchez is the best!)

Ben, Chrisie and Kev (for your support on this book), Sarita and Alberto (for making Pookie and Tushka real!), the "Russians"; Lilia, Emma, Vova, Alik, Roma, Dima, Grisha, Lera, Valerie and even Maryann ☺ (for being my family), and to the friends that once were part of my life, but now are gone …

Patticita (for giving birth to Ethan! ◉), Nicole (for your marketing advice ☺), Paolo and James (for helping me through a tough time), Christopher,

To all my friends: Maricesita (for ALWAYS believing in me ~ ya vamos a ser millonarios ☺), Evita (for being so sweet), Vinnie (for being my wild bud ☺),

ATOP THE WORLD, FAR, FAR AWAY,
WHERE WINDS ARE COLD AND NIGHTS ARE LONG,
A LITTLE PENGUIN SANG ALL DAY.
WHEN HAPPY OR SAD, HE SANG A SONG ...

... BUT HIS SONG CARRIED SO MUCH ACHE,
THAT ONE NIGHT HE LOOKED HIGH ABOVE,
AND WISHED TO FIND A WAY TO MAKE
HIS SONGS LESS SAD AND FULL OF LOVE.

On a white, cool summer day, somewhere in the magic Icelands, a penguin named Pookie and a polar bear named Tushka found a surprise in the sea.

"Look, Tushka!" Pookie said. "There's a little blue piano in the sea!"

Tushka scratched his head, confused. "What's a piano?" he asked.

"A piano is a great instrument," Pookie replied with joy. "With it you can make lots of songs ... lots and lots of happy songs!"

"Yaaay!!!" Tushka raised his arms in excitement and jumped up and down happily.

Pookie smiled hopefully and said, "I'm going to jump in and rescue the little piano!"

Aurora

"But what if, what if ..." Tushka said raising his arms high in the air, "when you go into the sea ... you find a big blue monster-fish!!!"
"What will you do if it tries to eat you?"
"What will you do? What will you do?"

Pookie smiled at Tushka and said, "Monster-fish are not real, so you shouldn't be afraid. But even if I were to find such an incredible fish, maybe he wouldn't try to eat me, maybe he'd want to play with me."

"But are you sure ...?" Tushka asked worried.

"Yes, I'm sure," Pookie replied.

"Oh ... okay then," Tushka agreed, and with relief, the bear smiled.

Pez-Monstruo

4

Pookie dove into the waters and swam with his strong flippers. He quickly reached the little piano and pushed it towards the little bear.

Tushka rushed to help Pookie and grabbed the edge of the little piano. Tushka pulled **hard** and then pulled **harder** … and with a loud **plunk!** … the little piano came out of the water.

Pookie and Tushka pushed the little piano towards their precious House of Ice.

"Pooookieee, I'm tired," Tushka whined. "I can't push this anymore."

"We're almost … there," Pookie said catching his breath. "We have to … take the little piano … to the cellar. Then I'll make … a small fire … to melt all … the ice away."

"But what if, what if ..." Tushka said raising his arms high in the air, "the fire grows hotter and larger ... into a big orange monster-fire!!!"

"What will you do if it tries to burn you?"

"What will you do? What will you do?"

Pookie smiled at Tushka and said, "Monster-fires are not real, so you shouldn't be afraid. But even if a large hot fire grew inside my little house, we would quickly run outside where the fire couldn't reach us."

"But are you sure ...?" Tushka asked worried.

"Yes, I'm sure," Pookie replied.

"Oh ... okay then," Tushka agreed, and with relief, the bear smiled.

Pookie and Tushka tried to push the little piano downstairs. But the ice that encased the little piano was much bigger than the doorway.

Little Tushka closed his eyes and took in a big long breath. Tushka pushed **hard** and then pushed **harder** … and with a loud **thump!** … the frozen piano went down the stairs.

Pookie made a small fire and placed the little piano close to it. He then told little Tushka to stay away from the fire. Tushka nodded in agreement and sat next to his friend, and while staring at the flames, the little bear fell asleep.

After a couple of hours, Tushka woke up from a scary dream. Pookie calmed him down and then told him, "The ice has melted! Let's play the little piano!"

"But what if, what if ..." Tushka said raising his arms high in the air, "when it's dark, the little piano ... turns into a big red monster-piano!!!"

"What will you do if it tries to bite you?"

"What will you do? What will you do?"

Pookie smiled and then he said, "Monster-pianos are not real, so you shouldn't be afraid. But even if the little piano turned into an amazing monster, maybe he would be a nice monster, and he would make music for us."

"But are you sure ...?" Tushka asked worried.

"Yes, I'm sure," Pookie replied.

"Oh ... okay then," Tushka agreed, and with relief, the bear smiled.

Pookie and Tushka carried the little piano to their spacious living room. Then Pookie smiled at Tushka and said, "I'm going to play happy songs for you!"

"Yaaay!!!" Tushka raised his arms in excitement and then he quickly sat down on a chair.

Pookie gently pressed the piano keys and caringly tried to make music. At first the little penguin made mistakes, but soon he remembered how to play.

Pookie's songs were very pleasant … but he noticed, with disappointment, that no matter how much he tried, he could play only sad songs.

"My turn! My turn!" Tushka yelled, as he rushed towards the little piano.

Tushka hit the piano keys and eagerly tried to make music. At first the little bear was happy, but soon he knew something was wrong … he wasn't making any music … he was making an awful noise.

So, Tushka tried hitting the keys **hard** and then much **harder** than before … but Tushka noticed, with surprise, the sound somehow became much worse.

The little bear burst into tears. "I can't make music," Tushka cried.

"You just need to practice," Pookie told him.

The little bear chewed on his necklace as tears ran down his cheeks.

Pookie wanted Tushka to be happy, but Tushka was too little, and pianos are hard to play.

Pookie then had an idea. "Come with me!" he told his friend.

"I have a gift for you!" Pookie told Tushka as he ran up to his bedroom. "This is for you," Pookie said and gave Tushka a little red drum.

Tushka wiped his tears away and held the little drum in his arms. He then scratched his head and asked, "How do I play the little drum?"

Pookie held up two wooden drumsticks and then told his little friend, "Hit the little drum with these sticks, and while you do that, just have fun!"

Tushka gently hit the little drum and timidly tried to make music. At first the little bear had no rhythm, but soon he noticed, with excitement, that he wasn't making awful noises … he was creating a pleasant beat!

"Look at me, Pookie! I'm playing music!" the little bear yelled happily.

"Yes, you are!" the penguin said, and filled with hope he added, "Let's play together, my friend!"

Pookie played the little piano, this time following Tushka's beat. And while playing, Pookie noticed, his songs were different somehow.

… they seemed faster … maybe even nicer …

Pookie then suddenly realized: His songs no longer sounded sad!

Pookie could now play happy songs, and he knew the reason why.

… it was not because of the little drum …

… or the little piano they had found …

Pookie could now play happy songs, because he was not playing them alone. This time he shared songs with a friend … with a good friend … a friend he loved.

ATOP THE WORLD, FAR, FAR AWAY,
WHERE WINDS ARE COLD AND NIGHTS ARE LONG,
A LITTLE PENGUIN AND HIS FRIEND
WHEN HAPPY OR SAD, PLAY A NICE SONG ...

Cool facts about

The Arctic Region
(Known by Pookie and Tushka as the **Northern Icelands**)

The Arctic is an **ocean surrounded by continents.**
The Arctic Ocean is frozen.
Most areas are buried under 10 to 20 feet of ice.

The **North Pole** is located in the Arctic Ocean.

The Arctic's temperature is usually between 0 and 20 degrees Fahrenheit (–18and –7degrees Celsius). During the winter some areas (like Greenland and Siberia) can get **as cold as -90 degrees Fahrenheit** (–68degrees Celsius).
During the summer the continental area can get as hot as 90 degrees Fahrenheit (32 degrees Celsius).

The Arctic has been populated for about 20,000 years.
It has a **population of about 15 million people.**
The Inuit people live in the Arctic.

The Arctic is **owned by eight different countries:** Canada, Denmark, Finland, Iceland, Norway, Russia, Sweden and the United States of America.

In the North and South Poles th
During the **summer it is always ligh**

the Icelands™

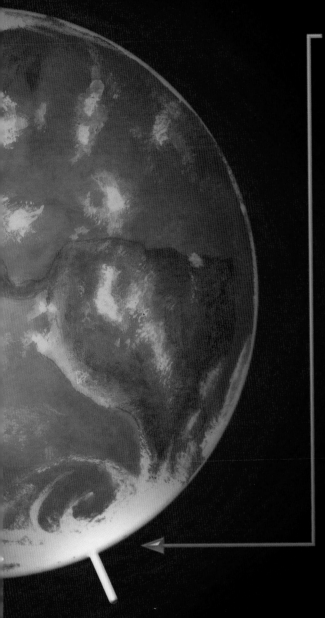

The Antarctic Region
(Known by Pookie and Tushka as the Southern Icelands)

Antarctica is a **continent surrounded by oceans**.
Antarctica is covered by an ice cap.
Some areas are buried under 10,000 feet of ice!

The **South Pole** is located in the continent of Antarctica.

Antarctica's temperature is usually between −20and −60
degrees Fahrenheit (−29and −51degrees Celsius) and it
is the **coldest, windiest, driest place on Earth**.
The lowest temperature ever recorded on Earth occurred
in Antarctica, and it was **−132 degrees Fahrenheit**
(−91degrees Celsius).
Antarctica is even drier than the Sahara Desert.

Because of Antarctica's extreme weather, no people lived
there until 1897 when the first explorers arrived.
No race of people permanently lives in Antarctica.

The Antarctic is considered to be **internationally owned.**
Many nations have claims on pieces of the continent
and often send research scientists to explore it.

ays and nights last 6 months each!
uring the **winter it is always dark.**

Illustration of the Peruvian Penguin (also known as the Humboldt Penguin).

Cool Penguin Facts

Penguins are **birds**.

Their feathers are white on their bellies and black everywhere else. Their **feathers act as camouflage underwater.**

Their favorite food includes: fish (especially anchovies), squid and krill (a small crustacean similar to shrimp).

Penguins walk awkwardly on land and can't fly , but they are **excellent swimmers, effectively flying underwater.** When tired of walking, they lie on their bellies, push with their feet and steer with their wings. This is known as "tobogganing".

Although most penguins can hold their breath for only a couple of minutes, penguins spend most of their lives in water. The Emperor penguins can **hold their breath for 20 minutes!**

There are **18 different types of penguins.** The Emperor penguin is the largest of all, standing 3 $^1/_2$ feet (1 meter) tall. The Fairy penguin (also known as Little or Blue penguin) is the smallest, standing 16 inches (41 centimeters) tall.

Penguins **live ONLY south of the equator:** Antarctica, Australia South Africa and South America. Penguins don't live in the Arctic.

**So, if penguins and polar bears live in opposite ends of th
Well, that's a stor

Cool Polar Bear Facts

Illustration of the White Bear (the name given to Polar Bears in Russia).

Polar bears are **mammals.**

Their fur looks white because it reflects light from the snow, but in reality, their **hairs are transparent and hollow!**

Their favorite food includes: seals, walruses, birds, fish, seaweed and grass.

The polar bear's **paws are well designed to walk on ice.** Their thick claws stop them from slipping. When the ice is very thin, they crawl on their bellies to keep the ice from breaking.

Although Polar bears spend most of their lives on the ice, they are great swimmers. They can **hold their breath for about a minute.**

There are **8 different types of bears.** Polar bears are the largest of them. Polar bears measure around 8 feet (2 $^1/_2$ meters) in length, but newborn cubs are the size of a guinea pig!

Polar bears **live ONLY in the Arctic.**

...orld, how come Pookie and Tushka live in the same place!?
...or another time ...

Learn more Cool Facts at:
w w w . p e r s . c o m

POOKIE Y TUSHKA
18 · 8 · 2002